Published by Parragon in 2011

Parragon
Queen Street House
4 Queen Street
Bath BA1 1HE, UK

ALICE
in
WONDERLAND

PaRragon

Bath · New York · Singapore · Hong Kong · Cologne · Delhi
Melbourne · Amsterdam · Johannesburg · Auckland · Shenzhen

One bright, sunny afternoon, a young girl named Alice found herself trapped with a history lesson. Whilst her sister read of ancient kings, Alice crowned her cat, Dinah.

The day was simply too splendid for lessons, thought Alice. As soon as she could, she slipped away from her lesson.

'Oh, Dinah,' she sighed, 'in my world there would be no lessons. All would be nonsense.'

As Alice dreamed of her wonderland, a well-dressed white rabbit ran past.

'I'm late! I'm late!' the White Rabbit said.

Alice raced after him. 'I wonder where he is going?' she said to Dinah.

They followed the White Rabbit to a rabbit hole. Alice squeezed through, even though she knew she didn't belong there. 'After all,' she said to Dinah, 'Curiosity often leads to...TROUBBBLLLE!' Alice's voice disappeared down the dark hole with the rest of her.

Suddenly, Alice was floating through the darkness! She thought she could see some strange objects falling along with her.

Through the gloom, Alice could just make out a lamp, and reached out to switch it on. Light flooded the tunnel, and Alice looked around in amazement. A book, a bottle, a picture, a candlestick—why, there was a whole household hovering around with her!

Alice dropped right through it all, and landed upside-down on the ground.

Alice saw the White Rabbit disappearing through a door in front of her.

'Oh wait Mister Rabbit, please!' cried Alice.

As she ran to follow him, she found herself passing through a series of doorways, each one getting smaller and smaller.

'Curiouser and curiouser!' Alice said.

At the very end she found a little door. When she tried to open it, the Doorknob said, 'Sorry. You're much too big.'

'Sorry. You're much too big.'

'Why don't you try the bottle on the table?' the Doorknob suggested.

A glass bottle appeared on the table, labeled 'Drink Me.' Alice took a sip, and immediately shrank down to tiny Alice! But she was too little to turn the key. A magic cookie made her big Alice, but then she was too big to fit through the door!

Her huge tears filled the room like an ocean. Alice shrank herself again, and floated through the door.

A wave swept Alice into a very odd race.
On a beach, some fish and birds ran round a Dodo,
trying to get dry whilst the waves kept them wet.

Alice spotted the White Rabbit again, washed up
on the beach just ahead of her.

'Mister Rabbit!' Alice called, running to catch up
with him. 'Please wait!'

Alice caught up with the White Rabbit at a small cottage in the woods.

'I'm late!' said the White Rabbit, 'go inside and fetch my gloves.'

Alice went inside the little cottage, and found many strange and wonderful items. On a table, she found a box of cookies labeled, 'Eat Me.' Happily, Alice helped herself.

Suddenly, Alice felt herself growing...and growing, and growing!

Alice grew so large, her arms and legs stuck out of the doors and windows!

'Help! Monster!' cried the frightened White Rabbit, and ran off to get the Dodo. When they came back, the Dodo suggested smoking the monster out by burning down the house!

Luckily, Alice reached down and ate a carrot from the Rabbit's garden, which turned her into tiny Alice again.

Running after the White Rabbit once more, Alice puffed, 'Oh dear, I'll never catch him!'

'Help!
Monster!'

Alice ran out of the garden, and came across a caterpillar making smokey vowels.

'Who are you?' the caterpillar puffed, making a smokey 'U' in the air.

Alice blew the smoke away, and blew the caterpillar right out of his clothes! She was worried, until she realized he had become a butterfly.

As the new butterfly flew away, he told her, 'One side of the mushroom will make you grow taller, and the other will make you grow shorter!'

Alice broke off two pieces of the mushroom. 'I wonder which side is which?' she said. With a shrug, Alice bit into the first mushroom piece.

Alice sprouted up through the trees, and caught a bird's nest in her bow!

'I'm terribly sorry!' she said to the angry mother bird. She had to get back to her normal size!

Quickly, she bit into the second mushroom piece, and then just licked the first piece.

Normal-sized again, she continued to look for the White Rabbit.

As Alice puzzled which way to go, she suddenly heard singing.

Looking up, she saw a Cheshire Cat sitting in a tree, smiling at her. 'If you'd really like to know,' he said, 'the white rabbit went that way.' He pointed down a little path.

The Cheshire Cat tipped his brow and said 'Of course, if I were looking for a white rabbit, I'd ask the Mad Hatter. Or the March Hare. Of course, he's mad too. Most everyone's mad, here.'

Alice walked on until she heard more singing. That must be the Mad Hatter and the March Hare, she thought.

The tea-for-twosome were wishing each other a 'Merry Unbirthday', and Alice joined them at the table. The Mad Hatter whisked off his hat, and there was an unbirthday cake! 'Make a wish!' he said to Alice.

As if in answer to her wish, the White Rabbit appeared! 'I'm late!' he said, as the March Hare and Mad Hatter tried to fix his watch with jam and sugar.

Alice shook her head and walked away. 'I've had enough of this nonsense,' she said.

'A very merry unbirthday!'

Alice got lost in the woods. The Cheshire Cat appeared, and opened a door for her, into the world of the Queen of Hearts.

Alice soon learned that everyone was afraid of the Queen.

The White Rabbit raced into the court to announce the arrival of the Queen. That's why he was worried about being late, Alice realized. No-one would want to be late for the Queen.

'Her Imperial Highness, the Queen of Hearts!' called the White Rabbit.

The Queen of Hearts spotted Alice.
'Why, it's a little girl!' she exclaimed. 'Now, where are you from, and where are you going?'

'I'm trying to find my way home,' Alice answered.

The Queen puffed up angrily.

'YOUR WAY!' the Queen shouted. 'All ways here are MY ways!'

The Queen calmed down when she learned that Alice played croquet. The Queen loved croquet, and challenged Alice to a game.

The cards always made sure that the Queen won every game of croquet she played. The Queen didn't like to lose.

As she lined up her shot, the Cheshire Cat appeared. Only Alice could see him.

'You know, we could make her really angry,' he said, as the Queen prepared to swing.

'Oh no, please don't!' cried Alice, but he tangled up the Queen's skirt as she swung.

As the Queen flopped down, the skirt flopped up!

'Someone's head will roll for this!' the Queen cried as she heaved herself up. 'Yours!' she bellowed, pointing at Alice.

'Couldn't she have a little trial first?' the King said to the Queen. She harrumphed, but said yes.

The White Rabbit read the charge: Alice had caused the Queen to lose her temper.

'Are you ready for your sentence?' the Queen asked Alice.

'Sentence? Oh, but there must be a verdict first!' replied Alice.

'Sentence first!' bellowed the Queen. 'Off with her head!'

Alice found the mushroom pieces in her pocket and stuck them in her mouth. She grew, and grew, until she towered over the Queen.

The scared King and Queen told Alice to leave the court.

'I'm not afraid of you!' said Alice.

Suddenly Alice felt herself shrinking!

'Off with her head!' the Queen cried once more. The court of cards closed in on Alice.

Alice raced away, into a maze. 'Which way?' she thought.

When she escaped the maze, she found herself back in the Dodo's beach race.

The Queen and all the cards were chasing after her. Ahead, she could just see the little doorway she had come through.

The Queen of Hearts, the March Hare, and everyone she had met chased Alice down the beach.

She saw the caterpillar again, and through his plumes of smoke Alice ran as quickly as she could to the little door, and tugged on the Doorknob.

'I simply must get outside!' she said to the Doorknob.

'But you are outside!' the Doorknob said. Alice peered through the keyhole.

There she was, sleeping in the meadow where she had heard her history lesson!

'Alice!' Alice's sister woke her. 'It's time for tea!'

Alice blinked, and looked around her. Her wonderland—with it's angry Queen of Hearts—was gone.

Alice shook away her dream, and smiled. This day was simply too splendid for nonsense!

'This day is too splendid for nonsense.'